Angels

By Jai Chewe

Published in the USA by:
Towne Woman Creations
P.O. Box 5872
Bloomington, Illinois 61702-5872
www.Townewomancreations.com

Printed in the United States of America
ISBN   978-0-9981499-0-5 (paperback)
            978-0-9981499-1-2 (hardcover)

Book & cover design by Darlene Swanson • www.van-garde.com

*In memory of
Carole Robertson,
Carol Denise McNair,
Cynthia Wesley, and
Addie Mae Collins.
You are all dearly missed.*

Contents

Acknowledgements

I'd like to give a huge thank-you to my mother and father, who have supported me through anything and everything. I'd also like to thank my graphic design specialist, Darlene Swanson; my editor, Jody Amato; and my illustrator, Tiana Scott, for how nice and helpful they have been. And my publishers, what would I do without them!

I'd also like to acknowledge my sister, Mia Chewe, for teaching me to speak my mind and to always be my true self. And lastly, to all of you guys for inspiring me to keep pursuing my dream of becoming an author.

Part 1:
Making Plans

oday was an unimaginably beautiful mid-fall afternoon. The kind of day you could imagine only in your dreams. Crisp leaves—all deep red and orange, tinted yellow-green, and burnt-sienna brown—dancing wildly and crunching with every step you took. Today was undeniably that type of day, and I wanted to spend it with my best friend in the whole wide world.

Momma, can I please go to Salei's house after lunch?" I asked. I was starving because it was already 12:45 and we usually had lunch at 12; the aroma smelled like sweet mashed potatoes, grilled chicken, and stuffed shellfish peppers.

"Sweet mashed potatoes, grilled chicken,

and stuffed shellfish peppers. It will be ready in about five minutes, so go wash your hands. I've already set the table," she answered, just as I had guessed.

I hurriedly scrambled toward the nearest bathroom when I heard Momma scream, "ALEX SIMONE BRANLEY!"

"O-ok Momma, s-s-sorry." I suddenly felt desperate for a lesson on how to speak English. I sounded like a child who was one or two years old, not a young girl of thirteen. My mother was seriously terrifying when she scolded me. It made me feel like the time when our family was caught in a severe thunderstorm when I was five. I had been so scared, I felt like I was on the verge of wetting my pants.

After lunch, I hurried (not running) down the hallway and into my "perfect," "spotless" room. As I frantically began making my bed, I thought to myself, Why don't I use my record player? So I trotted across the

room and placed a Bobby Darin record on my record player, and started back to my bed as I hummed "Beyond the Sea."

About three minutes later, I was done making my bed, and headed out the door. Once the screen door closed, I sprinted across the dewy grass, getting my pink sneakers soaked with sticky, pollen-filled water. It made me think about the times Salei and I had raked up the leaves from the front of our houses, put them in front of her house, and hurled ourselves into them! That was hilarious, but we got scolded for it because Salei's Dad had to rake all of it up.

Once I got to Salei's house, we both strode down the hall and into her room when she blurted out, "We should go somewhere."

"Where should we go, Salei?" I asked shortly.

Well, I was wondering if you wanted to go with me to the Baptist Church up the street and watch the quire girls perform. Do you want to come with me?" Salei answered.

"Sure! I bet my mom will think that it's going to be a great 'bonding' experience for us. Your mom could just drop us off there and we can watch! Nice one, Salei!" I gave her a high-five because I was truly excited about this.

We rushed down the hallway to inform Salei's Mom about our idea, and to my surprise, she said yes! After that unusual action, Salei's Mom called Momma and asked if I could go, and it was even more surprising when she said yes too! As soon as we heard the news, Salei and I jumped up and down rapidly in excitement.

SALEI

I was so excited! Alex and I were going to the performance! At first, I didn't think that she even wanted to go, probably because our favorite song is "Beyond the Sea." But I didn't want to get too carried away because she may have been unexpectedly busy on Sunday. I mean, it was only Wednesday.

I only went to the radio after Alex left my house because she completely hated it. All that I listened to was the news. Since segregation had just been banished, some of the whites were frustrated with the whole thing. I turned the radio on and heard the speaker say: "Black folks, this is a warning: stay in your homes and latch your doors tight because the Ku Klux Klan is here. They are marching down streets, invading public areas, and blowing up buildings. Save yourselves from these evil people!" I turned the radio off quickly and ran across the street to warn Alex. We could not go to the Baptist Church!

ALEX

I heard a knock on the door down the hall. I shuffled from my room to see Salei at my front door. She had a very worried look on her face; I knew that it was bad news.

As soon as I opened the door, she started talking. "Alex, we cannot go to the Baptist Church on Sunday, it's too dangerous for us!"

"Salei it's going to be fine," I explained to her calmly. "It's a church—how dangerous could it be?"

"No it won't, Alex! The KKK is here and they are at all kinds of different places!" Salei interrupted in hysterics.

"Salei, news flash! Segregation is over and has been over for weeks now. We're free!"

"You know what, Alex, you're right. Segregation is over. Why would the Ku Klux Klan still be coming to Birmingham, right?" Salei questioned softly.

"Exactly. So don't get head over heels with this stuff, the KKK isn't here anymore. Go back to your house and lay down, I think you're getting delusional or something."

Part 2:
The Day of the Performance

SALES

As I was putting my dress on, I thought about Wednesday's news on the radio, but I didn't hesitate. Alex had told me that everything was going to be okay, and I needed to learn to trust her.

I went outside and started speed-walking to Alex's house, but I found her already on her rocky driveway, beaming her perfect teeth toward me.

As soon as she saw me, Alex marched over and hugged me really tight. "I'm so excited! So, is your mom ready?" Alex asked.

"Yea, let's go," I answered.

As soon as we got into the lobby of the Baptist Church, I got really excited. People were one of the many enjoyable things in my life.

ALEX

I felt like I was unable to move. I just couldn't believe we were actually going through with this!

"BOOM!" Everything went completely dark.

SMILES

"What's going on? Alex, Alex! Where are you? This isn't funny, Alex!" I yelled. Just then, I felt an unbearably painful pounding on my body. Screaming in pain, I had suddenly figured out what was happening: I was dying. When everything came back into focus, I quickly tried to stand up and looked down to see my body under a boulder.

ALEX

I was in so much pain, mostly from my head, but it suddenly stopped after a few minutes. I looked around slowly, expecting the pain to come rushing back in a couple of seconds, but it didn't. In front of me I could see a rock lodged into my neck and forehead. I knew that I was dead, or dying.

SALEI

I sobbed loudly, thinking about the future that Alex and I could have had together. How she was going to have to live without me. But then I heard my name being shouted out by a familiar voice, "Salei! Salei where are you?" Alex was dead too.

I sprinted as hard as I could to her, cold tears streaming rapidly down my face. She spotted me, and we both stopped dead in our tracks, staring into each other's welled-up eyes. Everything around me faded away.

"Salei."

"Alex"

"I'm dead," Alex whispered.

"Me too," I blurted.

Both of us hugged each other and sobbed.

Part 3:

Angels

ALEX

I saw the bodies of Salei's and me lying on a gurney as the doctors rolled us away, along with four other girls. They had been in the choir. And instead of watching them perform, I was watching them lay on top of each other, lifeless. I felt so badly for everyone; we all had so much to live for. I should have listened to Salei. We should have stayed inside of our houses. If it weren't for me, we would still be alive right now I would never forgive myself for this. Never.

SALEI

Our parents found Alex and me at the hospital, I tried to talk to my mother, but she couldn't hear me. People who are living cannot speak to angels and expect to hear a voice back in response; only the unexplained happened to the people. I would never be able to verbally communicate with the world ever again.

ALEX

Salei and I walk down the busy hallway of the hospital, searching for our bodies. I saw the four girls again, and I suddenly gasped when I spotted a rock jammed into one of the girl's foreheads. In front of me, a gurney sped by with a little girl coughing up soot and covering her bloody eye. I saw Salei staring at her too, and then she looked forward and started running at top speed. She needed to see what they were doing to us.

SALEI

I bolted, then Alex followed. Alex and I ran down a few rooms until she stopped suddenly and pointed. I looked to see my and Alex's bodies lying together. And when

I looked over, I saw my mom, dad, and my little brother, Francis. I stumbled to the wall, slid down, and covered my face as I cried loudly.

ALEX

Momma and my dad huddled over me, tears streaming down their faces, and I screamed so loud, Salei looked up from where she was crying by the wall. Banging on the glass door, I screamed out words that I could no longer understand. Salei was no longer crying, but whining.

She slowly stood up and shuffled over to the window, leaning on it like she could no longer hold her weight. But surprisingly, she fell through the door and landed flat on her face. Wait a minute—angels can walk through walls? I wanted to test it out, so

I walked to the back wall and ran through the door, tripped on a wobbly Salei, and fell on her head.

"Ouch! Alex, what was that for? Are you crazy?"

"I was trying out the walk-through-a-door thing, but you tripped me when I ran through." I explained. Salei should've gotten up from the floor before I came zooming in.

"But you didn't exactly walk, did you?" Salei sharply replied.

Salei

I stood up and crossed the floor to my body. It's kind of odd how dead (or unconscious) people look. So peaceful, and even the rudest person can look completely innocent. Walking steadily to Alex's body, I thought the exact same thing. Yet, she looked a little more terrified than me. I glanced up to spot Mrs. Branley. I touched her, but the only thing that she could feel from me was a draft.

"Excuse me?" Mrs. Branley sniffled. "Can you turn the temperature up a bit, please?" So she did feel it.

Alex

I carefully stood up and walk over to Salei's body, "You look so peaceful, yet you are frightened by something. Why Alex?" she asked me.

"I was frightened at the fact that you were going to lose me. I was frightened at the fact that we were going to lose each other. That is my biggest fear in the whole wide world, losing the people that I love. But I know that if one of us survived, we would never forget each other, we love each other way too much," I answered.

"I love you too, Alex, and I could never spend a day without you in my life knowing that you may never come back. I'm glad that we are getting through this together, I'm glad that I am doing this with you. This is the reason why we are best friends; we rely on each other. That is how it was and how it always will be," Salei smiled softly.

SALEI

Alex and I walked out of the hospital with no emotion. All that we wanted to do was help our city with the great despair that just happened. "Alex, do you think that we should start helping out in the city?"

"Yea, this isn't something that Birmingham is going to get over too quickly or easily. Especially the African-Americans like us. But how are we going to fulfill that, Salei?" Alex asked.

"Well, you know how angels make blessings, or protect you from bad things? We could protect the city from the Ku Klux Klan. Then Birmingham will be blessed. Right?" I answered.

"I think so," said Alex. Alex is really smart so I was pretty sure that she was correct. "Oh, Salei, you know what angels do? They can put thoughts in people's minds. Maybe when the police department starts their investigation, we could make them think the correct thing. That the KKK bombed the church." Alex's ideas were so much better than mine.

Part 4:
The Investigation

ALEX

Salei and I got a cab ride (with the cab driver unknowingly driving us to the police station) downtown to the station where it was loud with buzz from the bombing a few hours earlier.

Hey, Alex, how about that one?" Salei pointed at the muscular man in his mid-thirties with an FBI badge on his chest. Perfect, I thought, I bet he could beat down the Ku Klux Klan.

"Yea, he's the one," I told Salei.

"Which one of us should do it?" Salei wondered.

"Both of us. But not today. Maybe we should give them some time; maybe to investigate it ourselves."

Suddenly, everything went white. Then I saw a heavenly figure. It was GOD!

He said, "Do not do this, my children, for I shall give them my blessing, but carry it down to you.

Very quickly, a light flashed through my vision, then everything went back to normal. Except everything was not normal…But we went to the police station anyway.

A man passed by me, newspaper in hand, and I checked the date: May 17, 2000. Wait … May 17, 2000!

"Salei, we aren't in 1963 anymore, it is 2000! We were in heaven for thirty-seven years!" I shouted out frantically.

Uh oh, we need to go tell the police that the KKK blew up the Baptist Church! At least the station isn't far away." I looked behind me, and to my surprise the police were exactly where they were in 1963. I tapped Salei's shoulder and she looked at me with a puzzled expression.

"What?" she asked.

"Look behind you," I answered in awe. Salei turned around slowly in silence. When she was facing the police station, she couldn't catch her breath and her mouth dropped wide open.

SALEI

I found myself walking into the station with Alex and giving my blessing to a thirty-five year-old police officer who was still strong.

He finally blurted out, "Since we know who the witnesses are and what the killers look like and that they are the splinter group Cahaba boys, the only thing we need to do is narrow it down to the features of the two men. We can disguise ourselves so that they won't suspect the FBI. And there it is!

"So agents Gale, Terry, Alan, Brown, Carter, and I are going to disguise ourselves as Klansmen and arrest the terrorists." The whole station applauded and cheered. The five FBI members walked to where the officer stood.

"Good idea, Agent Frances!" one of the
policeman shouted. The officer's name was
Agent Frances, interestingly.

ALEX

We followed the six FBI officers to where
they were going to arrest the two terrorists.
They looked terrifying in their KKK uniforms.
But seriously, who sells Klan cloaks? Salei
and I pass all of the unfamiliar men; we

stared like they are aliens from outer space in front of us.

We remembered so many things that weren't there anymore and it felt extremely weird … especially the clothes that people wore. They all looked very modern.

Once all of us got to the triple-K meeting destination, I was beginning to doze. It had taken us about an hour and forty-five minutes to get there.

"Ugh," mumbled Salei.

"I know exactly how you feel. I didn't know that it would take this long to get here," I was beginning to get impatient.

All of us got out of the car. All Salei and I could see where white robes and pointy hoods. They were all cheering and laughing … it was almost too much. The FBI joined them. The six of them blended in perfectly. A tall, skinny man stood up on what appeared to be a podium in front of a huge

cross. All the men gathered around, then the whole crowd fell silent.

"My fellow Klan members, it has been another great year with you all and another great year of protests. Our father, Nathan Bedford Forrest, is very, very proud of us. Yet we are still in secrecy. Our victory is endless in the past years and years to come. But we wouldn't be so victorious if it weren't for our act in 1963. Everyone, give a great hand to Herman Cash and Bobby

Cherry!" the man announced proudly. All of the men applauded and made a huge space so the two men could be seen completely.

The six men nudged through the crowd to "congratulate" them. Salei and I followed.

"Good job, you two. I am very proud of you," Officer Brown smiled. He and Officer Terry stood behind the men and patted them on the back. Quickly, the both of them took out their handcuffs and arrested the two; yet nobody heard the jingling sound of the cuffs.

"FBI. You are under arrest for the murders of Carole Robertson, Addie Mae Collins, Carol Denise McNair, Salei Carter, Cynthia Wesley, and Alex Branley. You have the right to remain silent," Officer Brown said. The two officers nudged Cherry and Blanton to the car as the other FBI members followed, along with Salei and me.

SALEI

We actually did it ... God, I want to thank you endlessly for helping us catch the bad guys. We are ever so thankful for it.

ALEX

Thank you, God, for giving us the greatest blessing ever. I will always love and appreciate you endlessly. The bad guys are gone forever. I am so grateful ... no, Salei and I are ever so grateful. Thank you!

SALEI

Robert Chambliss, Thomas Blanton, Bobby Cherry Herman Cash were given life sentences in prison for mass murder, hate crimes, white supremacy, and terrorism. Bobby Cherry is deceased and Thomas Blanton was denied parole now, but this act of hatred still lives on today as one of the cruelest crimes in history.

A memorial was built in honor of the four innocent girls who were killed: Carole

Robertson, Addie Mae Collins, Carol Denise McNair, and Cynthia Wesley. The 16th Street Baptist Church still stands today and is a symbol of African-American strength.

This story is based on true facts of what happened in Birmingham, Alabama. Alex Branley and Salei Carter are fictional characters, and a tribute to all those who were injured or killed during the Civil Rights Movement.

THE END

Jai' Alana Chewe
Child Author

Jai' Alana Chewe is an intelligent and outspoken twelve-year-old whose once-hidden talent for words has come to light, much to the delight of her readers everywhere.

With her wide and wonderful imagination, Jai' was drawn to writing at an early age. What started as a school assignment turned into her very first children's book, *The Jazzi Club.*

Once *The Jazzi Club* was published and made available online, Jai' began receiving invitations for book signings at local public events. All around her central Illinois town, people were excited to meet the young author who published for the first time at the age of nine.

Jai' has become an inspiration to everyone who believes that anything is possible. She is a role model for girls her age and has a growing audience of admirers and supporters.

Ever the driven young lady, Jai' isn't ready to stop with one book. . . she is determined to write many more! She continues to write story after story in the privacy of her room.

When she isn't writing, Jai' enjoys reading and playing volleyball. She loves learning new things and expressing what she thinks and feels about the world through words.

Jai' lives in central Illinois with her parents and sister, Mia. You can find out more about Jai' at www.facebook.com/Jaichewe/.

www.ingramcontent.com/pod-product-compliance
Lightning Source LLC
Chambersburg PA
CBHW020624120726
47905CB00003B/933